Little Bird Stories

Volume Eight

Selected by Michelle Winters

Little Bird Stories

Volume Eight

Invisible Publishing
Halifax & Picton

Cataloguing data available from Library and Archives Canada

Cover and interior design by Megan Fildes | Typeset in Laurentian
With thanks to type designer Rod McDonald

Printed and bound in Canada

Invisible Publishing | Halifax & Picton
www.invisiblepublishing.com

We acknowledge the support of the Canada Council for the Arts which last year invested $20.1 million in writing and publishing throughout Canada.

Canada Council   Conseil des Arts
for the Arts   du Canada

ABOUT THE CONTEST

I LOVE CREATIVE EXPERIMENTS. Magic happens when artists are at play.

When I first opened a Twitter account in 2010, I tweeted daily writing prompts, just for fun. They worked so well that people wanted to know how to use what they'd written, which is where the idea for The Little Bird Writing Contest came from.

It's now an annual, international contest exclusively for innovative short fiction writers.

This year, I created one special story prompt for everyone. I wanted to see what would happen when different writers from around the world were challenged to write from the same spark.

The 2018 contest prompt was:

Start your story with a balloon that has an unusual message. Use the words "lemon" and "ecstasy" somewhere in the story. End the story with an electrical storm.

When you ask a writer to take you on an adventure, you'd better be prepared for a surprise!

We had a tremendous variety of stories in response to the prompt. Michelle Winters has selected three excellent stories for the anthology this year — three new voices, each one very different. Each one is stunning.

I hope you love the results of this creative experiment. May the reading be as much fun as the writing!

Sarah Selecky

THE SHERPA WITH SNACKS

IF YOU THINK OF READING AS A THRILL-RIDE into the unknown (and I hope you do), the right guide on that journey can make all the difference. A good writer acts as a capable companion into whose hands you deliver yourself, the way the great Anthony Bourdain surrendered himself to local cuisine. It's more fun when you don't resist. But in order to fully abandon yourself to the experience, you need to trust that your guide has your enjoyment and best interests at heart. In reading these stories, I was looking not just for a Sherpa with a flawless sense of direction, but one who also brings snacks.

Writing is an act of expression, sure, but it's also an act of empathy. You're giving a piece of your soul to the reader; you want to make sure they're enjoying themselves while they're consuming it. Make sure they have everything they need. Let them know you value their time and intelligence, because while they could be reading anything, they've decided to read you. Make them laugh, wring their hearts like a sponge, show them something they've never seen. Be worthy of their trust.

All 147 of my guides showed me fascinating places filled with zesty lemon wonder, cryptic balloons of hope, and looming black clouds of human complexity. They showed me despair and redemption, and I've emerged, as one should, with my psychic and emotional molecules scrambled in the very best way.

This was not an easy decision to make, but in the end, it came down to hosting skills. These are the stories that really busted out the good China and white gloves for the sake of the reading experience. They were confident and inventive, took extra care with character and pacing, and added a little extra emotional impact for the ride.

"Things Float Away" doles out its bitterness with a sure and steady hand. It's a series of razor-sharp incisions cutting deeper and deeper to slowly reveal the calamity of getting what you want. The repeated appearance of the pink shirt (O, the pink shirt) is just one of the emotional landmines lying in wait throughout. But it's the timing of the last line that made this story so brutally satisfying. The way the writer juxtaposes it with Tara's recollection of the day at the beach with Rob makes it an absolute punch in the face. Special mention goes to the moment Tara lays on the floor and lifts up her shirt under the skylight "to feel the hot floor on her back and the sun on her belly." We do strange things when we're alone.

There's a precision to the writing of "To Weather a Storm" that I wish I could describe as something less punny than "surgical," but there you have it. The voice is swift and efficient—the only way to write about a character like Dr. James Parkes. The author's use of lists is a nice, clean way to establish the impeccable order of everything in James' control, laying the structured groundwork for the moment things spiral out of it. Once you recognize the stakes, James' singlemindedness becomes contagious, making you as anxious for the fragile Lyla as he is, and making you feel just as empty and helpless at the end, as he faces his own ineffectuality. The creeping dread and human frailty nail it for this one.

I was hoping "Sorry I Was Such a Dick" would live up to the boldness of its title—and it did. It was brazen and original, with a strong narrator, with a strong intention. You can really feel it when a writer is ensconced in a character and is showing you the world through those eyes. That's what I felt with this narrator. Every moment is utterly true, because it comes through this incredibly believable young woman we know almost nothing about except the deep truth of what she shows us. There's no writer to be found here, which is a tremendous feat. I believed every word.

I'm a sucker for redemption, and when it hits here, it's touching and identifiable (I, for one, have been that jerk), while faithfully retaining the caustic humour of the narrator. I laughed out loud more than once, and that's why it's my top pick. Writing funny takes a whole other level of skill and consideration, and I sometimes worry that we, as writers, forget about it. When a writer takes the time to make me laugh, I feel compelled to express my gratitude. So thank you.

Please enjoy these excellent stories. You're in very good hands.

Michelle Winters

SORRY I WAS SUCH A DICK
ESTHER GRIFFIN

NEXT IN LINE IS THIS DUDE, old, like probably thirty, and he's still got his sunglasses on. He clears his throat and croaks at me. "So, ah, I heard you can fill up balloons, even if I didn't buy them here."

"As long as they're helium-quality. Sure." I ignore the lady third in line waving at me like she's some kind of priority. Katie's an hour late for her shift, so I'm the only one on cash.

"I bought these online. I don't know." He tosses three red balloons on the counter.

I take a look at them, not able to make out the tiny white printed message. It's hard to tell their quality, so I recite the Party-Hut-non-guarantee. "Because it wasn't purchased here, I can't guarantee it won't pop, and if it does, Party Hut won't compensate."

He half nods, half grunts. "How much to fill it?"

"$1.79 a balloon."

"For air?"

"Helium. And the service."

"Jesus fuck. That's highway robbery. Just give me the one." He grabs the other two back and pulls some change out of his pocket.

"What colour ribbon do you want?"

"Green, so it looks like a rose." He jingles the change in his meat paw. "It's for my girlfriend. We had a fight." Total overshare.

I place the balloon on the nozzle and pinch it extra hard so it squeals as it fills. I try not to piss myself laughing as it inflates and reads *Sorry I was such a dick*. This guy's a real winner. "That's two dollars. Would you like to donate to children's charities today?"

He slams a toonie on the counter and takes off.

"All the best with that." I say it to his back, the balloon bobbing behind him like the shittiest apology I've ever seen.

The next customer dumps out a basket of ten for a dollar candies, and I start counting.

"There's 250. I already counted." She chews her gum like a camel.

"I still have to count it."

"Whatever. Hey, don't you go to Central High too?" I recognize her. A low-key ecstasy dealer who hangs out with the smoker skids at the side door.

"Yep." Customers don't realize that if they shut up, it will go a lot faster.

"Wanna come to a rave tonight? I'm in charge of the candy." She winks at me. "I can hook you up."

"Pass." No way I'd touch her sketchy shit. "Would you like to donate to children's charities today?"

"Sure. Five bucks." Her eyes are a little too shiny. "Ooh! Nerds." She grabs two boxes of grape/strawberry and tosses them on the counter.

I ring her through and hand her the bag. "Next!"

Suddenly the waving lady is in my face. "Excuse me?

Did you not see I was waving to you?"

"I was helping another customer."

"But I just had a quick question."

I give her a slow death blink. "How can I help you?"

"Do you have those gender reveal balloons?"

"Yes."

"Well, I'd like to buy one. It's a girl!" She opens her sweater and shows me her bulging belly.

"So you *do* want to make a purchase, not just ask a question?"

"Well, I guess." She hauls her huge purse onto the counter and starts digging around in it. She pulls out a lip gloss and rings her lips until they're dripping. It stinks like rancid berry. "How does it work?"

"It's a black foil balloon filled with pink or blue confetti." Total gender-typing bullshit, if you ask me. "You pop it at the party."

She claps her hands like some kind of deranged seal. I point to the packages on the wall behind me. "Single or party package?"

"What's in the package?"

"Five balloons. One foil reveal balloon and four smaller ones." I toss it on the counter so she can read it. My manager, Judy, shuffles by, gesturing for me to smile. I pinch one off for her and look at the clock. Only four more hours and then I can blow this place off for good. I love these seasonal gigs. After the deposit, I've saved enough in my pug fund to afford my puppy, Sir Pugglesworth. Eight weeks old and he's finally ready to bring home. The wait has been brutal.

"I'll get the package then."

"Name and email." She glares at me, and I know what's

coming. Like a hundred times a day I hear this shit.

"Why do you need my email?"

"To place the order."

"But you can't just fill them up now?" She puts her hand on her hip.

"Not for a package. It'll be a twenty-to-thirty minute wait."

"But you just filled up that other guy's balloon."

"It was a single. Do you want a single instead?"

She shakes her head. "Fine. I guess I'll have to wait then." She rubs her stomach and actually gives me a pouty face, like some fetus is going to melt my heart.

"Name and email."

"I said I'll wait."

"I can't enter the balloon order in the system without an email."

"I am not giving you my email." The guy behind her groans. He's lugging two baskets full of luau shit and looks ready to wail.

"Then I can't place your order."

"I want to speak to your manager."

"Sure thing." I press my walkie head piece. "Judy, please come to the front for customer service." I give her my most syrupy smile. Fake it 'til you make it, like Grams always says.

Judy's voice crackles in my ear. "It'll be five minutes."

I turn back to Princess Preggers. "She'll be up in a few minutes. Wait over there please." I jam my thumb to the right.

"I don't want to lose my place in line."

I lean past her. "Next!"

I ring through another three customers while she gives

me the death glare, like five minutes is going to kill her. She should try being an hour overdue for break, waiting on a slacker coworker to show her ass.

Judy doddles up to cash and tells the lady the same shit I told her.

"Fine, but you really should teach your employees some manners. She's a very rude girl." She cuts back over in line and spits her email address at me. This gets me burning. Like, seriously, I'm rude?

"Can you arrange them for me?" She looks at me like I'm some kind of florist.

"No. We don't provide that service."

"Some party store."

"Do you want to purchase a bag for a dollar?"

"A bag? For inflated balloons?"

"It makes them easier to manage and transport."

The woman laughs. "I don't think so."

"Would you like to donate to children's charities today?"

She just ignores me, so I ring her through.

"I'm going across the street and I'll be back in twenty minutes." She taps her relic wristwatch and says it again real slow to get it through my thick skull. "Twen-ty min-utes."

"Next!"

Katie finally shows up, looking dank. "Rain's started."

"Fuck, Katie. I'm way overdue for my break."

"My rat's sick." She scratches at her acne and gives me a sad shrug.

"Sorry, man." Scribbles is the best, so I can't stay mad at her. She sets up her till and calls the next customer over.

Judy waves the gender reveal balloons at me. "Can you get started on this order for me before your break? I just have to do a return and I'll be right back."

Everyone in line looks longingly at me like I'm going to stay on till. I turn my back to them and tear open the gender package. I look at it for a good few seconds, then think, what the fuck. My contract's over today anyway. I stuff the reveal balloon in my apron and pick a generic black foil balloon from the bulk bin. Keeping my hands out of sight under the counter, I grab a handful of poo emoji confetti. I funnel it into the balloon, keeping my eye on the aisles. I inflate it and tie it off just as Judy comes back over to relieve me. A deep growl of thunder sounds and the lights flicker.

"Sounds like a doozy coming. Go take your break already." She winks at me.

On my way downstairs to the break room I stuff my pocket with a handful of lemon warheads from the candy carousal. I pop one in my mouth. "That's the shit."

The lights keep flickering, and I hope to hell the power doesn't go out when I'm in the dungeon of a break room. Last time that happened the generator failed, and I had to grope my way back upstairs. As I walk down the birthday party aisle, I notice the ceiling is starting to leak again, so I slide the bucket under the drip.

My break isn't long enough to go anywhere, so I chill with my snack and pull up photos of Sir Pugglesworth on my phone. He's the cutest little dude you could ever meet. Thirteen hundred dollars and worth every penny and every dull hour of work. I get to pick him up on Saturday. Grams took some convincing, but she said if I could afford him, she'd help feed him.

I'm just finishing up my ketchup chips when Judy comes in and sits down at the table with me. She looks all serious so I figure I'm busted. It's not really how I'd planned to go out, but I needed to show Princess Preggers what rude really looks like.

"We need to chat," she says.

I nod, racking my brain for some kind of excuse. I settle on denial. A factory defect.

"So, we're looking for a part-time fall supervisor. You interested?"

I just stare at her. Grams used to always say it's the dickheads who get ahead in life.

"It's eighteen bucks an hour. Evening shifts and weekend to work around school." The lights flicker again. "We think you've got good potential."

I start adding up all the extra cash. The dog treats. Puppy training. That cute matching harness and leash I saw online. Nothing but the best for my little dude. "Sure. Count me in."

"Great. Come in on Monday for training, and we can sign the contract then."

I nod and a serious puke-wave comes over me. It's been about twenty minutes. "Hey, thanks Judy." I get up and sprint up the stairs through the baby crap aisle. Princess Preggers isn't there. I run up to the balloon pick-up carousal and see her order is gone. The store has thinned out a bit, but I don't see her anywhere.

I figure I have to confess, so I head back to the staff room. But then she comes around the paper plate aisle and heads for the exit. The automatic doors open and the winds grabs her hair first, tossing it around in her face. The rain is coming down sideways. She struggles against it, and her balloons twist on their ribbons in a frenzy and pull in all different directions. The rain's coming down hard, and if it wasn't so fucking hilarious, it would be a tragic sight.

The thunder rumbles loudly and the lightening flashes after only one Mississippi. I wonder for a second if lightening would be attracted to foil, so I start over to her. Before I get there, she yells, "Oh no!" as her balloons take flight. She jumps up and down on her tippy-toes, belly bouncing, as if that's going to help. She turns and sees me and hangs her soggy head. Her shirt is soaked, and there's something about how her belly button is poking out in my direction that give me an uneasy feeling in my own stomach. I wave her over to cash.

"I just wanted it to be perfect," she says. She's trying not to cry. "The baby's almost here. Waiting for her to arrive has been so hard."

"Yeah." I take her over to the side counter and fill a new package for her. I get the balloons all snug in a bag, on the house. "Hold them here." I show her how to pinch the strings just below where they're tied on. "And you'll be fine."

THINGS FLOAT AWAY
TRACEY MCGILLIVRAY

TARA OPENS THE DOOR for the delivery man just as the wind catches his hat and blows it across the front porch. "Whoops!" he says, watching it go. His hands are busy holding two long white boxes adorned with raffia bows and a bright yellow balloon. The name of the florist circumnavigates the balloon's equator.

She studies the swirly font. Fleetfleur. Not bad, she thinks. Implies you'll get your order promptly. The French adds a touch of class. And the alliteration makes it memorable.

The balloon bats at the man's head like a punching bag. He tries to give her the flowers but she stoops to retrieve his hat. Their words stumble over each other. "Here, let me. Oh, thank you. No, thank you!"

Tara closes the door and stands in the cold hallway, listening to the comforting chug of the washing machine on the second floor. She carries the boxes to the kitchen and drops them on the island. A small white card drifts to the counter. *Happy Anniversary*, it says.

Two dozen? For Pete's sake. She'll have to find her largest vase. She can't remember the last time she saw the sharp trimmers with the yellow handle. Are they in the garage or the garden shed?

She sighs. Twenty-four stems to cut. Then rummage through the box for the square plastic packages that always make her think of condoms. Shake the white powder into lukewarm water and watch it settle to the bottom.

Yesterday she found a long-forgotten arts-and-crafts project in Bobbi's toy box. It must have involved balloons and plaster of Paris, but it had broken down and adhered to dozens of the expensive building blocks that Bobbi loves.

Tara wanted to dump the entire mess in the garbage. Instead, ever the frugal farm girl, she spent the afternoon scrubbing bits of blue rubber and white cement from every single block.

She slides the raffia off one of the boxes and peeks inside. Red roses, laid to rest on white florist's paper smooth as silk. The balloon lolls sideways on the counter, only the first half of its label visible.

Her cell phone rings and displays a New York area code. She turns away without picking it up.

Once the flowers are dealt with, she goes upstairs, shifts towels into the dryer and starts a load of jeans. The washing machine was out of commission for a few days last week and she's still catching up. She shakes her head, remembering how hard it was to find someone to look at it.

The young repairman who finally came had an accent that provoked a surprising flutter in her stomach. She left him to his work and went to make beds. When she came back she found him on his hands and knees, wiping water off the floor with his shirt. The shirt had been hiding strong shoulders and a defined torso. A swimmer's body.

"Oh!" she said. "Let me get you a towel."

"Just a splash," he said. "Had to swap a hose."

She managed to keep a straight face until he left. Then she collapsed against the door, faux-fanning her cheeks and making a mental note to tell the story next time she has lunch with friends. For the first time in ages, she felt buoyant.

They moved here a year ago but she has yet to call it home in her heart. She misses their old house, despite its tilted floors and drafty windows. It's where they nested. Where two became four. She often thinks fondly of the bitter February night the furnace broke down. They all clambered into the king-sized bed, cuddling and whispering, then dozing off in a drift of homemade quilts.

Now that Rob works in New York, she lies alone on his side of the bed, to be closer to the phone in case of an emergency. She wears an old pink T-shirt that used to be his. But she doesn't sleep well.

Last night a man in a white robe and a long beard walked into the bedroom and stood over her. Then he climbed into the bed and sat, silent, on her chest. He was so thin, almost emaciated, but his weight was unbearable.

When she woke up she couldn't move. Her lungs burned, demanding air.

Eventually she got out of bed, made the girls' lunches and drove them to school, but she's still fighting a nasty dream hangover. Tara pauses on the bright, warm landing at the top of the stairs. What does it mean that this, a place meant only for passing through, is her favorite spot in the whole house? The skylight above her illuminates a perfect rectangle on the floor. She closes her eyes, and the heat from the sun, intensified through the glass, reminds her of a perfect beach day.

She spent her teenage summers working at an ice cream shop by the lake. Her parents had sold the farm by then and moved to town. She could hop on her bike and be at the beach in less than fifteen minutes. On days off, a whole gang of her high-school friends played volleyball and sipped beer from cans wrapped in plastic covers that, if you looked close enough, said Peppy Cola or Spite.

Some of her friends dated tourists, but Tara refused to. She dealt with too many spoiled rich boys at the ice cream store. They always had money for double scoops and took forever to choose their flavours. When she bent over the freezer to reach the bottom of an almost-empty tub, scooping in the efficient figure-eight pattern her boss had demonstrated on her first day, she was sure they were staring at her butt.

The summer she turned eighteen, one of her friend's cousins came to spend the summer. Rob had the same messy blonde curls as Dale, but his eyes were the palest blue she'd ever seen, like they'd absorbed enough light to illuminate a lifetime. When Dale introduced them, Rob took her hand and shone those eyes on her. She felt her insides being scooped clean. She immediately granted him landed immigrant status.

They were enrolled in different universities for the fall, but by August they were researching bus schedules so they could visit each other.

Someone once asked how they made it work, those four years apart. They'd looked at each other and shrugged. That was the plan.

After graduation, they both found jobs in Toronto. They bought a used car, a cute red convertible that turned out to be a lemon. They collected stories about the many places it broke down, usually while overloaded with building supplies. Rob's father had loaned them money for a down payment on a bungalow and for months they spent every night and weekend working together: stripping faded paper from the walls; ripping up blue shag carpeting; refinishing hardwood.

One long weekend, they added a deck to the back of the house. The day they finished she took what has always been her favourite photograph of her husband. Rob, in red shorts flecked with paint and a T-shirt that had turned pink in the wash, grinning at the camera. At her. His arms spread wide, as if to say: Look what we did!

A few months later, she stared, stunned, at a blue line on a tiny strip of paper. She hadn't expected to be expecting the first month they tried. And when Bobbi was only nine months old, (surprise, again!), Tara got pregnant with Addie.

She's grateful they can afford her staying home. But she loved her marketing job, and always thought she would go back, at least part time, when both girls were in school. Then last year, the same month they moved, Rob was offered a promotion too good to turn down.

"It will mean two days a week in New York," he said. "But it's such a quick flight."

"Of course," she said. "You have to take it."

Two days a week have grown to four, sometimes five. The flights from La Guardia are often delayed by thunderstorms. Last weekend Rob didn't make it home until Saturday morning. Then he spent hours on the phone, waving at the girls to keep the noise level down.

When he left Sunday evening, Rob stood at the door with his briefcase and and called goodbye.

"Bye, Daddy," said Bobbi and Addie, almost in unison, without looking up from their colouring. Tara saw the stricken look on his face and thought, Well, what do you expect? Aloud she said, "Girls, go hug your father."

Tara drops to her knees in a doorway of light in her lovely, lonely house. She strokes the sand-coloured hardwood, then lifts her shirt and lies down to feel the hot floor on her back and the sun on her belly.

High above, strands of cirrus unravel like cotton batting against the hard, blue sky. She conjures the sounds of rolling surf, of insistent seagulls. She closes her eyes.

She dreams of the day she saved the world.

They were playing volleyball with an inflatable beach ball. The plastic was imprinted with deep blue water and dark green continents and they'd taken to calling it the world. It was late in the afternoon and they'd worked their way through a two-four that Dale had carried to the beach under his arm on his ten-speed.

"I'm king of the world!" Dale shouted as he spiked the ball. It was a wild shot. They all stood with hands on hips, panting, and watched the ball land outside the court. It bounced and rolled down the beach to the water's edge.

A gust of wind sent the ball into the waves and still they stood. "The world is floating away to Michigan," someone observed.

It was Rob's ball, but he hadn't grown up on the lake and didn't know how to swim. He shrugged.

"Things float away," he said.

His nonchalance infuriated her. That wasn't like him.

"Not if you don't let them," she said.

"Tara, don't worry about it," said Rob. She turned her back on him. She ran into the water until her wrists trailed lacy bubble cuffs. She dove in.

It took several minutes of hard swimming to catch up

to the ball. She was winded. The beer, she thought. She reached out to grab the ball but it spun away. She tried again and sent it skittering, blue-green-blue-green, across the tops of the waves.

To her right the dark concrete of the break wall marked the end of the protected area. She knew she should give up but couldn't stand the thought of going back empty-handed.

She chased the ball all the way to the deep, white-capped channel that ran between the harbour and Sandtree Island, the bird sanctuary. Tara's arms quivered with fatigue. Her precise stroke had become a halting windmill.

This is how it happens, she thought. It would be so easy to just stop. To succumb to the ecstasy of drowning. As if from a great distance, she watched her body settle to the bottom.

No, she whispered to the waves.

I want to be with Rob.

I want to have children and live in a beautiful house.

Please.

She kicked her feet one last time, reaching through the water to the underside of the ball. She cradled it in her palm and pulled it towards her, willing it not to blow away until she could wrap both arms around. There.

She clung to the world, taking ragged breaths.

Inside the break wall, the water was calmer. Tara floated on her back with her head toward shore, letting the waves carry her in. She would never tell anyone how close she came to giving up that day.

Rob splashed through the shallows, crying and laughing and shaking his head. "You stubborn, stubborn woman," he said. "What am I going to do with you?"

"Kiss me," she said.

The water tickles the back of her head as Rob drops to his knees. Before his lips reach hers, he disappears in a flash of lightning.

Tara sits up. Touches her wet hair.

Storm clouds moved in while she slept. Rain pummels the skylight. What time is it? She races to the bedroom but the clock radio blinks all zeros. Back in the hallway she slips in a puddle. What the hell?

Another flash of lightning reveals water streaming from the laundry room. The new hose has come loose. Bloody plumber. Tara finds the shut off valve and cranks it tight. She reaches for something to start mopping up the mess: a faded pink T-shirt.

TO WEATHER A STORM
SHOSHANA GERTLER

THE WIRE FALTERS, the monitor stutters, the balloon deflates, and James checks his watch. Half past two. Late. Beside him, wearing pink latex gloves because the standard blues dwarf his hands, the new resident eases the catheter back a few millimeters. Takes a moment to rub an itch on his forehead with the back of the wrist peeking out of his glove. On screen, James watches the thin wire withdraw. My god, this is a thirty-minute procedure, a minor blockage of a minor branch of the coronary artery. James takes in a loud breath, half a sigh, but catches himself before its release, catches the kid resident's stiffening shoulders, the nervous sidelong glance, and lets the air out a bit at a time, silent.

"You were there," he says, and his voice keeps even. "Re-inflate the balloon." Two thirty-two. He has to call the sitter at three.

The kid stammers a response, guides the catheter back in, raises his thumb over the inflation device—"Use the dye," James reminds him, this time with words pinched and impatient—and then, after releasing the iodine to watch the blood branch across the monitor, he expands the balloon a second time. A pause, another uncertain eye dart toward James.

Oh, for goodness—"Give it to me."

James shoulders the kid aside, replaces pink gloves with his own steady hands. At this pace, the patient will die of old age before anyone leaves the cath lab.

He releases the pressure and injects more dye to inspect the newly widened space. Two last puffs of the balloon, another gush of iodine to test for vessel perforation. Simple.

The kid edges back toward the table with a stammered, "Er, sorry, doctor," to reclaim his post for the finale. James plants his feet so that, in a moment, the boy gets too close, has to backtrack with a little stumble. James ignores him and in seconds has removed from the patient's thigh the balloon-tipped catheter.

He unwraps a square of gauze and, mockingly, hands it to the kid. "Think you can apply pressure?" he says—not a question—and grinds his teeth when the kid answers, "Yes, doctor."

By the time James is cleaned up and back in his office, his watch reads 3:15. Someone left a Thermos on his desk, recent, it's still steaming, and when he picks it up the bottom leaves a ring of condensation on the lacquered wood surface. Laid neatly beside it, a folded napkin and a stirring rod from the cafeteria. James peers out to the corridor, catches the eye of his appointment manager—young, barely out of college, but competent, oh, competence, what a commodity— and raises the Thermos in toast. She nods.

After he unscrews the lid, a burst of steam warming his face, he tucks his office phone between ear and shoulder. Dials the sitter's cell, long ago memorized, while his free hand gropes inside his desk drawer. His fingers close around a bumpy round shape at the exact moment that a tinny voice says, "Hi, Mr. Parke."

He doesn't care at all to correct the title. On top of the desk, beside his Thermos, he sets down the small green fruit that rolled around in his drawer all morning. Truth, he prefers lemons, doesn't care for extra tartness, but the only thing he found in the fridge this morning was the lime. That and a jug of lemon juice, but that was concentrate.

He says the girl's name—Trish—as a greeting. He must apologize, he explains, for not calling at three, got held up, procedure ran long, how was Lyla?

"You know you don't have to call. We're great." He hears the smile in her voice, indulgent, and isn't that a tickle, a twenty-something nanny indulging the forty-plus cardiologist?

He waits for her to continue, meanwhile digging his knife—also from the drawer—into the rind. The blade slices neatly through the fruit's middle. "And Lyla?" he prompts, when the line is silent a number of seconds. He tucks half of the lime into a Ziploc to take back home tonight.

"She's napping." Still?

"Yeah, she had a rough morning."

James pauses. The remaining lime half is cupped against his palm, fingertips firm around the peel to keep it in place without puncturing the skin. He raised the lime above the Thermos to squeeze into his water, but now he lowers it again, un-squeezed, as a single droplet escapes down his inner wrist. It runs along his radial artery. Rough morning. He doesn't have to ask what that means.

For one breath, James closes his eyes and pinches thumb and forefinger together against the very tip of his nose, a small but sharp pain pushing everything else away. And then, he thanks Trish for the update, adds that he'll likely be home late but his wife will get back in time for Trish to leave at five—"I know, Mr. Parke"—and please call when Lyla wakes, just leave a message with his appointment manager.

There is a pause. "You really don't need to check in every day, Mr. Parke," she murmurs. "Lyla and I are fine." He thanks her again. Hangs up.

He stares for a moment at the sticky line of juice that traveled down his arm. With the corner of the napkin he swipes it dry. He squeezes lime juice, seeds and all, into his water and gives the mixture a quick swirl with the stirring rod. Two taps against the thermos edge, wicking off the excess liquid, then a long, slow swallow. Lips purse as it goes down—too sour, of course; he'll pick up lemons from the farmers' market on his way home. Avocados, too, for his wife.

He sees four patients that afternoon: one office visit (new referral), two inpatient follow-ups, and one consult requested by Neurology. Two get EKGs—the referral, with a likely diagnosis of acid reflux and an overly anxious disposition, and the consult, who also receives a cardiac monitor, because Berger up in Neuro usually has a keen eye for cardiac involvement. Of the follow-ups, the first is healing fine, a clean, tight line sewn down his sternum three days after surgery; the other is going to die. Probably not today. But by weekend, maybe into next week if the half-dead heart of an eighty-nine-year-old smoker finds some previously untapped resilience.

On his way out someone calls James's name in the lobby, a scuttling mess of face he doesn't recognize even after the guy, seeing James's blank stare, offers a name. James remembers him only when the guy says, "I'm the one—the, er, angioplasty? Earlier today?" James stares briefly at the boy's hands, no longer gloved but still more familiar than his face.

"Consider family medicine," James grunts, which—for all it makes the kid's face blanch—is much gentler than what he wants to say, Biology teacher, or even, Airport bagger. Incompetence, the greatest sin.

There's still daylight when he steps outside beneath the giant neon H of Hospital. Warm and humid and, as he crosses to the parking lot, lightly breezy against the back of his neck. On his way home, he picks up avocados and lemons, hits a spot of traffic on the highway, and still makes it back before 7:30.

He hears laughter, whooping bouts of it, as soon as he opens the front door. The guttural sound, to others unexpectedly deep, belongs to his three-year-old. James finds them in the kitchen, Shelly and Lyla together at the table. On the surface in front of them stands a plastic stick with a bird-shaped head, wearing, naturally, a top hat. Before it, a glass of water.

Lyla, refusing to use her booster seat, has propped herself up on her knees to watch the contraption. The plastic head rocks backward, a moment, a moment more, before diving beak-first toward the glass of water. Another delighted eruption from Lyla, and then she looks up at James to cry, "Daddy, Daddy, look what it does!" Ecstasy is so easy for children, even children like Lyla.

Lemons go into the fridge; avocados stay out to ripen another day. Leaving the empty paper bag on the counter,

James joins them at the table. Shelly turns her face upward to accept a kiss. Lyla, who has already lost interest in them, turns away again, exposing the red-brown tufts at the crown of her head, and James bends his face to it, the roots still damp and fragrant from bath time, and kisses her there.

An hour later, Lyla tucked in, James sitting in bed, Shelly steps out of the bathroom, robe tied, toweling her hair dry.

"I heard she had a seizure this morning," James remarks. He sets down on his nightstand the file he was perusing and looks up.

"Two, actually," Shelly replies as she climbs into bed beside him.

He closes his eyes. To blink, but then they stay shut like that for many long seconds until he feels a light pressure land on his chest. Her hand, James sees when he opens his eyes, and she is watching him from her pillow, waiting for him to speak. So James the doctor takes his wife's hand and presses her knuckles against his lips and tells her they will be fine. He will talk to Berger in the morning, ask—as if James hasn't already, how many times?—if she has any other suggestions. Maybe she knows some way around the restrictions on cannabis oil for minors. James will ask tomorrow.

How can the state not see, his wife demands. With all the research. "We'll be okay," he says again.

In the morning, because on Fridays, Shelly leaves early, James stays long enough to administer Lyla's meds. He arrives at the hospital to learn the ER admitted one of his longtime patients. Arrhythmia. Light-headed for months, collapsed for the first time yesterday. Didn't bother coming in until morning. "My grandson was visiting, Doc. Sixteenth birthday." She fishes a toddler's photo out of the purse on her bedside table. "He looks exactly the same," she coos.

Despite himself, James quirks a half smile. "Eleanor." She looks up. "You should have come immediately."

"Oh, piffle," she announces. "I'm here now." She is confident, she tells him, regardless of her negligence, that he'll get her right as rain. "Everyone says you're the guy who gets things done." Highly recommended, Dr. Parke, just not enough to heed his warnings.

He lets her show him one last photograph—her five children as teenagers—and, outside, jots a memo to find out which colleague can fit a pacemaker procedure into his schedule.

He tracks down Berger, who tells him everything about epilepsy he already knows.

He fields a call from a patient who's been waiting six weeks for a new heart—no, nothing yet—and stays on the phone while she begins to heave deep, gasping sobs, what should she do, her children are still young, she doesn't want to die, please, please. He tells her, "We're not there yet, Laura."

She asks, "So where are we?"

"We're at a cup of tea." He talks her through the brewing—"Do you have green tea?"—"Yes, why, is green good for hearts?"—"It's good for peace of mind, Laura." He waits until her first sip, until she calms to an occasional sniffle, then lets her go. "There's time."

He calls Trish at three, and Lyla is awake to tell him she saw monkeys at the zoo.

Before the day ends, he reviews treatment plans with the other cardiologists and both cardiothoracic surgeons. Jennings can squeeze in the pacemaker tomorrow, once Eleanor has fasted overnight.

Over the weekend, as predicted, the patient with a half-dead heart dies. The post-op patient is released with instructions for incision care and a prescription for pain. Neuro's patient has atrial fibrillation. Acid reflux guy has acid reflux. And James goes out for a picnic. (He "goes out" as far as the backyard, where he helps Lyla spread a check-ered sheet across the lawn.) The three of them lay out tuna salad, sliced avocados, and wedges of watermelon beside a pitcher of fruit punch clinking with ice.

It gets late, past Lyla's bedtime, but she wants to watch the sun dip behind the neighbor's rooftop.

"I took a nap, Daddy," she begs.

Shelly goes in to start the dishes, clear away some of the mess Lyla made carrying the bowl of watermelon outside, and James stands up with her to collect trash. The water-melon rinds he tosses into the bushes for some curious birds or squirrels to find; the punch in their cups he spills onto the grass. Lyla, grinning, lies back against the sheet. James collects their plates, their empty cups, and the glass pitcher and carries them inside. He sets the pitcher on the counter and the dishes by the sink.

When he returns for what's left of the tuna and avocados, Lyla's arms are bent sharply above her head, chin tilted back as if tracking the sun's descent, but her eyes are wide and blinking, blinking in a too-steady rhythm. Every limb, rigid, vibrates. Her hands are frozen half clenched into claws.

James goes to his daughter. He reaches inward, but James the doctor, James the man in control, pours through his fingers like sand. He is empty; he is nobody-James. Lyla's throat releases a strangled sound. Uh... ah... uh... James sinks to his knees at her side. Uh... ah... ah... One hand on her shoulder, the other beneath her back, he turns her onto her side and shifts her legs as best he can toward her chest to stabilize the position. He has no pillow for her head, but the ground beneath their picnic sheet is soft. He cannot hold her, wants to hold her, so he leaves his palm against the stiffened curve of her shoulder.

He shouldn't have let her stay up past bedtime. "Daddy, I napped," she'd begged, and that voice comes back now to mock him. His despair, the cardiologist's— it's something grotesque. James the doctor knows the tremors are a brain exploding, abnormal synchronous neuronal activity shooting across hemispheres, knows in a few seconds, a minute, she will go limp; stertorous breathing will replace this soundless squeak of air trying to pass through a taut trachea. He sees her spine arch, back, back. Does not see, but knows just as well, synapses fire beneath her skull. Knows he will be able to hold her as she comes to, disoriented at first, but awake, eventually aware, his Lyla. But the doctor has no power to retrieve her. And nobody—James, like his daughter, has been hollowed out, can only watch, hand slack on Lyla's rigid shoulder as the electrical storm rages, rages, while the cloudless blue sky bleeds into dusk.

Esther Griffin lives in Barrie, Ontario, where she teaches creative writing and English literature at Georgian College. She writes poetry, fiction, and graphic forms and is currently working on her thesis novel to complete her MFA in Creative Writing at UBC. Her poetry and fiction have been published in various anthologies. She can be found online at www.esthergriffin.ca.

Tracey McGillivray's nonfiction has appeared in the *Globe and Mail*, *Today's Parent*, and *Don't Talk To Me About Love*. She grew up on a farm near Lake Huron and, after completing an MA in Journalism, worked in health care communications. Tracey lives in Toronto with her husband, two teens and two dogs. "Things Float Away" is her first published fiction.

Shoshana Gertler is a fiction writer living in New Jersey. She began writing stories at the same time that she began reading them. In 2017 she earned an MFA in fiction at The New School in New York City. She has published her work in a handful of newspapers and magazines.

Sarah Selecky Writing School x Invisible Publishing:
Pocket books that celebrate phenomenal writing

The Little Bird Writing Contest is an international contest for innovative, emerging short fiction writers. The contest opens each spring when the birds come back and show-cases the excellent stories that come from **Sarah Selecky Writing School**'s daily writing prompts. Each winning story is chosen by a celebrated author and published in a beautiful anthology. Proceeds from anthology sales go towards the Pelee Island Bird Observatory and the Prince Edward Point Bird Observatory to help protect the real little birds out there.

Invisible Publishing produces cool and contemporary Canadian fiction, creative non-fiction, and poetry. As a not-for-profit publisher, we are committed to publishing diverse voices and stories in beautifully designed and af-fordable editions. Even though we're small in scale, we take our work and our mission seriously: we believe in building communities that sustain and encourage engag-ing, literary, and current writing.

For more information visit invisiblepublishing.com and sarahseleckywritingschool.com